Nathaniel Prentiss Banks

A Memorial of James Abram Garfield,

from the City of Boston

Nathaniel Prentiss Banks

A Memorial of James Abram Garfield,
from the City of Boston

ISBN/EAN: 9783744790239

Printed in Europe, USA, Canada, Australia, Japan

Cover: Foto ©Raphael Reischuk / pixelio.de

More available books at **www.hansebooks.com**

A

MEMORIAL

OF

JAMES ABRAM GARFIELD,

FROM THE

CITY OF BOSTON.

"Vita enim mortuorum in memoria vivorum est posita."

BOSTON:
PRINTED BY ORDER OF THE CITY COUNCIL.
MDCCCLXXXI.

In Board of Aldermen, October 31, 1881.

Ordered, That the proceedings of the City Council upon the death of James A. Garfield, late President of the United States, including the address of Nathaniel P. Banks upon his life and public services, be prepared by the Clerk of Committees, under the direction of the Committee on Printing, and printed for the use of the City Council, and that one thousand copies be issued; the expense to be charged to the appropriation for Printing.

In Common Council, November 3, 1881.

Concurred.

[Approved November 9, 1881.]

PRESS OF ROCKWELL & CHURCHILL, BOSTON.

CONTENTS.

ACTION OF THE CITY GOVERNMENT.

DEATH OF THE PRESIDENT.

JAMES ABRAM GARFIELD, President of the United States, received his death-wound from the bullet of an assassin, on the second of July, 1881, while in the Baltimore & Potomac railroad station, Washington, D.C. After eighty days of suffering, distinguished by heroic patience and manly endurance, he died at Elberon, N.J., on the evening of Monday, September 19, at thirty-five minutes past ten o'clock.

The news of his death was received in this city shortly after eleven o'clock, and the sad intelligence was communicated to our citizens by the tolling of the fire-alarm bells.

The Mayor immediately issued the following call: —

EXECUTIVE DEPARTMENT, Sept. 19, 1881.

To the Honorable the City Council of Boston: —

Having been informed of the death, which occurred this evening, of JAMES A. GARFIELD, the President of the United States, you are hereby requested to assemble in your respective chambers on Tuesday, Sept. 20, at 12 o'clock M., for the purpose of taking such action touching the solemn event as would appropriately express the sympathy of our citizens in this national sorrow, and their respect for the memory of the deceased.

FREDERICK O. PRINCE,
Mayor.

2

PROCEEDINGS OF THE CITY COUNCIL.

A special meeting of the City Council of Boston was held at twelve o'clock this day, in accordance with the call of the Mayor, for the purpose of taking appropriate action upon the death of the late President.

PROCEEDINGS OF THE BOARD OF ALDERMEN.

The Board was called to order by His Honor Mayor PRINCE, who read the call, and then spoke as follows: —

Gentlemen of the Board of Aldermen: —

It becomes my painful duty to give you official information of the death of JAMES ABRAM GARFIELD, President of the United States. Shot down by a base assassin, on the second day of July last, he lingered from that date until thirty-five minutes past ten o'clock last evening, when he died. During a large part of this time he suffered great pain, which he bore with manly and uncomplaining fortitude.

This terrible event has cast a shadow over the whole country. It has made a national sorrow. During all his long weeks of suffering the hopes and sympathies and prayers of the whole people have been with him, and now that suspense and anxiety are merged in grief and mourning they feel that the nation has lost a Chief Magistrate whose talents, experience, and patriotism were assurances that the great trusts reposed in him would have been well and faithfully executed.

Recently chosen from the people, by the people, to administer the government in their behalf, all the citizens, regardless of political differences or sectional divisions, were prepared to render him the loyal and generous support which he had the right to claim, and which our countrymen — ever subordinating party spirit to patriotic duty — are accustomed to accord.

We have every reason to believe that he would have so administered the government that every political and social right secured to the citizens and to the States by the Constitution would have been conserved, and that the progress of the Republic during his official term would have been such as to demonstrate the ability of a free people to select for their rulers those who are qualified for the grave and difficult duties of government.

They who enjoyed the privilege of his intimacy represent him as possessing, in an eminent degree, all those qualities of the head and heart which beget affection and attach men to each other; so that not only the nation mourns for the loss of a wise, sagacious, and patriotic magistrate, but the domestic circle and the large circle of devoted friends grieve for the loss of one whose kindly nature and great capacity for affection enabled him to discharge well and fully all the offices of friendship and all the obligations of natural relations.

The government of the country is never seriously disturbed by the death of any of its officials, however distinguished he may be for public or private virtues, because it is based on law, supported by free institutions, and protected by the loyalty of a patriotic people. However much, therefore, we grieve for the loss of this excellent President, we are permitted to entertain, in our great bereavement, the consoling reflection that no apprehension can mingle with the regrets with which we lay his mortal remains in their last resting-place, that danger will come to the Republic, that the administration of government will be impeded, or that our free institutions will be in any way imperilled through the death of a President. The assassin may murder an official, but law and government he cannot kill while patriotism survives, and the people recognize the obligations of moral and religious duties.

The destiny of nations and individuals is in the hands of Him who notes even the fall of the sparrow. We bow in submission to that Divine Will, which orders all things well. We may not clearly see how a great and public evil can work for the good of a community; but there are some lessons which all may learn from it. It should teach us humiliation, the purification of the heart, the resolve that in the future there shall be larger charity in our intercourse with each other, a fuller recognition of our moral duties, and a deeper interest in the religious education of the people. Political institutions based on the affections of the people, and representing patriotism, piety, and equal rights, will survive rulers and parties, and can only perish when the public virtues which called them into existence shall decline and pass away.

The Chair will receive any proposition which is appropriate to the occasion.

Alderman O'BRIEN said : —

Mr. MAYOR, — It is with the deepest sorrow and regret that I rise to offer resolutions in honor of the memory of the late President of the United States. A few weeks ago we all rejoiced, because it appeared to us at that time that the hand of the assassin had failed to accomplish its purpose; that our President would live to serve his country with that distinguished ability and patriotism that had marked his course since his entrance on public life. An all-wise Providence has willed it otherwise. Elected but a few months ago the Chief Magistrate of the nation, he had but just entered upon a career of usefulness to his country, when he was stricken down for no cause whatever.

Fifty millions of people now mourn their great loss. Fifty millions of people are shocked that a man could exist among them, could grow up among them, who would be guilty of so great a crime. Words almost fail to express our detestation of the act by which so distinguished a citizen has lost his life, and the country a Chief Magistrate who was honored and respected throughout the land. In common with our fellow-citizens in all sections of the country, we mourn our great loss, and honor his memory. With these brief remarks I now submit the resolutions of the City Council.

RESOLUTIONS OF THE CITY COUNCIL.

Resolved, That the City Council of Boston, in common with other communities in this afflicted land, has learned, with the profoundest sorrow, that the long and painful illness of JAMES A. GARFIELD, President of the United States, who was shot by an assassin on the second of July last, has now culminated in his death.

Resolved, That, by the untimely death of President GARFIELD, this country has sustained an irreparable loss; for in him were centred all those graces which the highest culture could produce, all that political wisdom which a varied experience in the council and the field could secure, all that knowledge of men and public affairs which extensive study and thought could suggest, which united to make him in reputation and in fact the most illustrious citizen in the Union.

Resolved, That President GARFIELD exemplified, by his varied and interesting experience from boyhood to maturity, the American idea of a true and lofty citizenship; and in his wonderful career he exhibited the limitless capacity which waits at the inception of life upon every citizen, no matter how humble his birth, if he be only faithful to his duty and to God.

Resolved, That, besides his public virtues, we recognize also with grateful feeling his personal qualities, as exhibited by his patience in suffering, his fortitude in pain, his manly utterances, his sweet affections, and his Christian faith, which have been so conspicuously displayed, and which have attracted to his bedside the attention of this nation and the warmest sympathy and prayers of all mankind; thus illustrating in his death, as well as in his life, the strength and courage of a noble, virtuous, and Christian character.

Resolved, That the members of the City Council, individually and collectively, extend to the afflicted family of the late President their warmest and most sincere sympathies in this sorrowful hour; and they desire especially to recognize that devoted affection, that saint-like tenderness, and that heroic fortitude, under circumstances of agonizing suffering, which the honored wife of the late President has exhibited in her unparalleled trials.

Ordered, That the Mayor cause the City Hall and Faneuil Hall to be appropriately draped, the flags to be displayed at half-mast upon the public buildings for a period of six days, and the bells of the city to be tolled during the hour set apart for the funeral of the late President.

Alderman HERSEY said : —

Mr. MAYOR, — I hardly know how to voice the feeling of sadness that pervades every heart consequent upon the sad intelligence that our beloved Chief Magistrate has ceased to live. During the weary weeks in which, without a murmur, he has borne the suffering and pain of his protracted struggle for existence he has become more and more endeared to this people, and each day has intensified our desire that he might live. Over this broad land, from fifty million homes, comes the sad cry of bereavement from a heart-broken, stricken people. Across the wide ocean, wherever a Christian people dwell, the sad intelligence has cast its gloom. Flashing along the wires that form a sympathetic cord uniting the continents are speeding the words of sympathy from every land, showing that our grief and loss are shared by the common brotherhood of man. Words can but feebly express our sense of sorrow. That in time of peace, with no exciting issue to influence the passions of men, an assassin's hand should deal the blow of death, escaped upon many a field of battle; that our beloved President, in the strength of his manhood, when he had but reached the summit of human ambition, should be stricken down, seems sad indeed.

But so it has been ordained, — the dread messenger of Death has knocked at the door of the Nation's Capitol, and all that love and human skill could do were unavailing to stay his progress. A Christian warrior has fallen; the sword that he drew in defence of human liberty and a nation's life lies forever sheathed in its scabbard; and he has passed on to that realm "where the wicked cease from troubling and the weary are at rest," to receive the glorious reward of those who fulfil well their mission here.

The resolves and orders were adopted unanimously by a rising vote. Sent down for concurrence.

Alderman VILES moved that the regular meeting of this Board, on Monday next, be dispensed with, as that is the day set apart for the funeral of our late President, and that when this Board adjourns it be to meet on Wednesday, the 28th inst., and that all orders of notice be made returnable on that day.

Adopted.

Alderman SLADE offered the following: —

Ordered, That a eulogy upon the life and public services of JAMES A. GARFIELD be pronounced at an early day before the City Council and the citizens of Boston, and that a committee of three members of this Board, with such as the Common Council may join, be appointed to make suitable arrangements therefor.

Passed, and Aldermen SLADE, TUCKER, and HERSEY were appointed on said committee. Sent down.

Alderman CURTIS offered the following: —

Ordered, That a delegation from the City Government, consisting of His Honor Mayor PRINCE, the Chairman and one other member of the Board of Aldermen, the President and two other members of the Common Council, be appointed to attend the obsequies of the late President of the United States at Washington.

Passed, and Alderman CURTIS was appointed on said committee. Sent down.

Adjourned, on motion of Alderman O'BRIEN.

3

PROCEEDINGS OF THE COMMON COUNCIL.

The members of the Common Council were called to order by their President, ANDREW J. BAILEY, Esquire, who read the call for the meeting, and spoke as follows: —

JAMES ABRAM GARFIELD, the twentieth President of the United States, is dead. The tired heart is still, and the patient soul has gone to its home. Eleven weeks of memorable trial have been added to our country's history, — weeks of pain and anxiety for every patriotic heart. Who of us will ever forget the deep horror which prevailed on receipt of the first news of the terrible outrage, felt to be not only against the man, but against the nation itself?

Who will soon forget the gloomy anniversary of our birth as a nation, or the hunger for favorable news from the stricken President? Then the first gleam of hope, the alternating hopes and fears of these bitter days of national anxiety, the shutting out of all hope, and the stern recognition that death must come. Vividly as it now seems to us it will stand out still more vividly in the future. Two strong characters have been blazoned on our nation's page, that will grow stronger and stronger the closer they are studied.

The noble wife, rising from all but a fatal sickness, and, with heroism and fortitude never surpassed, comforting, cheering, and sustaining her stricken husband. Never despondent, never discouraged, she will stand forever as the American idea of noble wifely devotion, and of heroic and womanly character. The respectful homage of mankind is hers, and the sympathy of a nation's sorrowing people are with her.

Our second martyr-President, elected to his high office through respect of his talents and admiration of his noble manhood, the patient courage, the cheerful and almost boyish disposition in the endurance of long and terrible sufferings, endeared him to the hearts of the people, and made him the loved President of the American people. Our hearts are sad to-day, and the gloom of this terrible calamity will not soon pass from the nation's heart; but these examples of American manhood and womanhood will gild the gloom, and add heroism and loveliness to American character. It rests with us, gentlemen of the Common Council, to take such action as will testify to the nation the appreciation of our community of this affliction, and our sympathy with the mourning family.

The resolutions and order passed by the Board of Aldermen were presented by Mr. HENRY PARKMAN, of Ward 9, and upon their being read by the President, Mr. PARKMAN said : —

Mr. PRESIDENT, — In moving the adoption of these resolutions I cannot but attempt to feebly express the feelings which I know animate the breasts of not only all in this chamber, but of every one throughout the length and breadth of this land, to whom the news has come of the fatal termination of the long and lingering illness, and that our Chief Magistrate is no more. For eighty days, hourly we have examined each bulletin as it brought to us news of the condition of the President of the United States, and we have alternated between hope and despair. During those eighty days we may say that we have been fused into one nation. Though elected to the position which he held by one of the political parties of this country, party lines vanished before the assassin's blow, and political differences were forgotten in our common grief.

JAMES ABRAM GARFIELD, who was shot on the second of July, at his post of duty, exemplifies to us, as has been appropriately said in these resolutions, the fact that any one of us, by force of character, may reach the highest post in the gift of our fellow-citizens. His career has been watched so long by his fellow-countrymen, and is so well known to every one in this assembly, that I will not repeat it. We all feel that the attack of the assassin was upon each one of us; but at the same time we must remember what Mr. GARFIELD himself so eloquently expressed upon the death of our first martyr-President, that, though our chief has been stricken down, "God reigns, and the government at Washington still lives." Though we may mourn for him as one of the best and noblest types of American manhood, yet we must endeavor to show respect for his memory by attempting to carry out what we think he would have desired. And, Mr. President, as you yourself have so well said, with regard to Mrs. GARFIELD, while undoubtedly there are many women in this broad land who, under the same circumstances, would have shown the same fortitude and spirit in their troubles, yet it has been given to this woman to show what our highest type of American womanhood is. She has stood the ordeal nobly, and we extend to her our most sincere sympathies. Mr. President, I move the adoption of these resolutions by a rising vote.

Mr. WILLIAM H. WHITMORE, of Ward 12, said:—

Mr. PRESIDENT,—I rise to second the motion, in the name of those of us who did not aid in the election of President GARFIELD. And with that preface the memory of that opposition forever ceases. As President, he was our President; the chosen head of the whole people; the visible sign of a nation's sovereignty; the object of the love and loyalty of every citizen. He has fallen a victim to the dangers of his post,— a martyr to his country, as truly as any of his associates who fell on the field of battle. Most fortunately not a suspicion can exist that the cowardly assassin has a confederate or a sympathizer. The political framework of our government stands to-day intact and admirable; our sympathy can be freely and justly bestowed upon GARFIELD as a man grievously afflicted, but for that very cause nearer and dearer to us now and always.

This community, proud of its loyalty, is a unit also in its affection for the fallen chieftain. From the moment of the first announcement of the dastardly act until the stroke of the midnight bell proclaimed the mournful end, a shadow has rested on every household. The spectre of Death has been with us, day and night, as though the first-born lay stricken in every home. Day by day we have watched the bulletins, to glean a deceptive comfort from hopeful words, or to sadly anticipate the day which has now come. Kings and nobles have faced the scaffold with a firmness which awakened the pride of their followers; but for two long months our heroic President has faced Death with a courage and composure greater than theirs; a richer memory to the citizens of this republic; a higher example for them to imitate.

I most heartily support the admirable resolution of condolence with his wife and family. It will never be forgotten that his wife was his truest friend, his unfailing supporter. The few respectful glimpses we have of the sick-chamber reveal her as that crowning glory of a man, a true wife. Well and fully has she struggled, only to remain to bear a weary burden for many years. Friends may forget, children may outgrow their passionate grief; but the helpmeet of the President's life can but mourn and wait.

In behalf of every household in this community, in the name of every happy family in the land, we tender her our sympathy, our prayers for that consolation which the hope of a blessed immortality can alone afford.

One last word: the miserable cause of this calamity still lives, to learn, in due season, the weight of a nation's curse.

It behooves us all to see that he receives his just punishment, not in hasty wrath, but by the inflexible force of a just vengeance. It has been said that "there is a divinity that doth hedge in a king." Let us prove that the affection of a mighty nation forever encompasses its elected chief, and that the sword of justice, inevitable and relentless, awaits whoever strikes at the Nation's heart.

The resolves and order were read a second time and passed, in concurrence with the other branch, by a unanimous rising vote.

An order came down for the appointment of a committee to attend the funeral of the President, at Washington. Read twice, under a suspension of the rule, on motion of Mr. NATHAN G. SMITH of Ward 21, and passed in concurrence. Messrs. HENRY PARKMAN of Ward 9, and FRANCIS W. PRAY of Ward 5, were appointed on said committee.

An order came down for a eulogy to be pronounced upon the life and services of President GARFIELD at an early day, and appointing a committee to arrange therefor. Read twice, under a suspension of the rule, on motion of Mr. JOHN B. FITZPATRICK of Ward 8, and passed in concurrence. Messrs. CHARLES E. PRATT of Ward 21, WM. H. WHITMORE of Ward 12, PRENTISS CUMMINGS of Ward 10, WILLIAM E. BARTLETT of Ward 15, and JOHN A. McLAUGHLIN of Ward 7, were appointed on said committee.

Adjourned, on motion of Mr. ALFRED S. BROWN of Ward 23.

MEMORIAL SERVICES.

4

MEMORIAL SERVICES.

The Committee of the City Council appointed to make arrangements for a memorial service, in honor of the late President, fixed upon the 20th of October as the time for holding the services.

The Honorable NATHANIEL P. BANKS, whose intimate acquaintance with President GARFIELD gave him peculiar qualifications for the task, was invited to pronounce a eulogy, and accepted the invitation.

Tremont Temple was selected as the place for holding the services, and the Tremont Temple Corporation tendered the free use of the building for that purpose.

The offer of the Boylston Club to furnish the musical portion of the exercises was accepted.

Among those to whom official invitations to attend the services were extended were His Excellency the Governor, and the members of his personal staff; the Executive Council; Heads of State Departments; United States officers — civil and military — located in Boston; the Judges of the Supreme, Superior, and Municipal Courts; past Mayors of the city; city officers and heads of departments.

The platform was appropriately decorated. A crayon portrait of President GARFIELD, drawn by Mrs. W. C. HOUSTON, was placed in front of the organ.

The services opened at eleven o'clock with a voluntary upon the organ, selected from "Judas Maccabæus," by Mr. GEORGE W. SUMNER.

His Honor Mayor PRINCE then spoke as follows : —

ADDRESS OF HIS HONOR THE MAYOR.

Fellow-Citizens: — The vicissitudes of human life and the mutability of human affairs are forcibly impressed upon us by the sad fate of our murdered President. A short time ago we saw him in all the pride of his vigorous manhood, full of hope and health and strength. Comely in person and in manner, the gaze of millions was upon him as he stood before the American people, a candidate for the highest honor which the republic can confer upon a citizen. Less than a year has passed away since he was elected to the presidency, and only a few months have gone since, with the benedictions and blessings of the whole country, he was installed in his high office and began to administer the great trusts reposed in him. And he so bore himself as to satisfy even his political opponents that he was well fitted to occupy the exalted place to which he had been elected. But while "his greatness is a-ripening, with all his blushing honors thick upon him," the angel of Death issued his untimely summons, and Murder served the mandate. Yet he died —

> As sets the morning star, which goes
> Not down behind the darkened west, nor hides
> Obscured within the tempests of the sky,
> But melts away into the light of heaven.

The people, in the midst of their exultant hopes, are suddenly filled with lamentation and grief. Finite intelligence cannot explain why this appalling change was permitted to be, for the assassination was wanton, unprovoked, and without cause. The mystery must remain unsolved until the solemn day when all secrets are revealed.

When we remember, however, that not his countrymen alone, but nearly all the nations of the civilized world, without regard to differences of race, religion, forms of government, customs or manners, tenderly deplored the death of our President, and condoled with the American people in their great bereavement, — an event unparalleled in recorded history, — can we not be permitted to indulge the belief that this general sympathy may mean that peace and good-will shall hereafter more largely inspire the nations? If it shall thus be, then perhaps the great sacrifice has not been wholly made in vain. The city government of Boston, as one form of expressing the sympathy of the citizens at this time, has directed a eulogy on the life and character of our martyred President to be pronounced on this day. It will become a record, for the instruction of the generations which are to succeed us, of lofty patriotism, of eminent public service, of heroic fortitude under the severest suffering, of the calmest courage in the face of death, of Christian resignation to the will of Providence, and of unfaltering faith in a glorious immortality. A distinguished citizen has been selected for the discharge of this grateful duty. His intimate acquaintance with the deceased, his knowledge of his moral and intellectual qualities, and his appreciation of his patriotic services, will enable him to speak fitting words of encomium. The part assigned to me in these memorial services is merely the introduction of the orator to the audience.

The BOYLSTON CLUB, under the direction of Mr. George L. Osgood, sang the following requiem mass by Palestrina:—

Kyrie eleison, Christe eleison!
Hostias et preces tibi Domine laudis offerimus,
Tu suscipe pro animabus illis
Quarum hodie memoriam facimus.
Fac eas Domine, de morte transire ad vitam.
Quam olim abrahæ promisisti
Et semini ejus!

Sanctus Dominus Deus Sabbaoth!
Pleni sunt cœli et terra gloria tua.
Hosanna in excelsis!

Benedictus qui venit in nomine Domini.
Hosanna in excelsis!

Agnus Dei, qui tollis peccata mundi,
Dona eis requiem sempiternam!

The MAYOR asked the attention of the audience while prayer was offered by the Reverend SAMUEL K. LOTHROP, D.D.

PRAYER BY REV. S. K. LOTHROP, D.D.

Almighty, Infinite, and Incomprehensible God, we bow before Thee as the Creator and Upholder of the universe. Thy power rideth on the whirlwind; Thy wisdom discerneth the hidden things of darkness; Thy goodness poureth into our hearts their gladness. To adore Thee is our solemn joy; to trust Thee is unfailing safety; to love Thee is peace eternal. Without Thee we are and can do nothing. Dependence upon Thee is all our strength. In the beamings of Thy glory is all our light. In prostrating of our will to Thy most holy will is our highest dignity and elevation.

Help us, O God, to prostrate our wills before Thy will. In this time of our national calamity and sorrow, may we be still and know that Thou art God; may we be humble, lowly, and penitent; may no doubt disturb, may no murmur escape, may no fear prevail. Reverently and gratefully recalling all Thy gracious ways, all Thy merciful deliverances and dealings with this nation in earlier and in later times, may we feel that our trials and our triumphs, our glories and our calamities, our days of grand and magnificent and our days of sad and solemn commemoration, alike speak to us of Thy wisdom and Thy mercy in the steps by which Thou hast raised us up and led us onward to a high place among the nations. Oh, help us, therefore, to mingle gratitude with our thoughts as we gather here this morning at the call and on behalf of our city to commemorate the late President of these United States, summoned by Thee from his high place on earth to the footstool of Thy throne in Heaven; and while we listen to the words of wisdom and of truth which Thy servant shall speak to us, portraying in all the beauty and grandeur of their proportion his life and character and service, may our hearts become more and more grateful for that life, that character, that noble example, that wonderful career.

We thank Thee, O God, that through Thy providence, and his own energy and noble purpose, the youth triumphed over all the obstacles of a lowly lot and pinching poverty, and limited opportunities; that he succeeded in the acquisition of knowledge and the development of talents and the formation of character, so that he became a scholar and teacher, wise and skilful, faithful in all the highest objects of education. We thank Thee that when the exigency of the country demanded, the scholar and teacher passed into the soldier, and carried into the arena of war, courage, bravery, skill, a spirit of self-sacrifice, a power of endurance, an energy of perseverance, and an aptitude and sagacity in military affairs that showed him to be alike competent to command, and worthy to be trusted and obeyed. We thank Thee that when he was called from the camp to the capitol, from the military to the civil service of the country, he exhibited in the halls of legislation a breadth and wisdom of statesmanship, a logic and eloquence of utterance, a large and comprehensive policy, that indicated the force of his character and his principles, and secured to him respect, confidence, and trust. We thank Thee, O God, that when through these qualities and Thy providence, and the will of the people, he was called to the highest honor the nation could confer, and to the grandest trust it could confide to his keeping, he walked forward to that position with mingled dignity, modesty, and meekness, and that during the brief time he was permitted to discharge the duties of his office he did so with a broad, comprehensive, and patriotic integrity of purpose. And above all, O God, we thank Thee, that when suddenly struck down by the hand of wanton folly and malignity, and left to languish week after week in pain and suffering, and alternate hope and apprehension, with weeping friends, an anxious nation, and an admiring world at his bedside, during all this period no murmur or complaint, no bitter thought, no harsh word, nothing unworthy of a noble soul, escaped from his lips, was written upon his countenance, or displayed in his manner; but all was calm and serene, cheerfulness, submission, trust in Thee, the exhibition of a Christian temper, and the mighty power of a Christian faith.

And now, O God, that the end has come, amid scenes and circumstances that make it glorious to him, but a loss and unhappiness to ourselves, we pray that Thou wouldst help us to gather up the lessons of his life and apply them to our own characters and consciences. The life of the boy, the man, the scholar, the teacher, the soldier, the statesman, the president and chief magistrate of a great nation, and, above all, and in and through them all, of a simple, pure, unaffected, sincere, devout Christian.

O our Father, we pray that his name, his fame, and his memory, while they abide a rich inheritance and holy consolation in the hearts of his family, — the wife and mother and children, whom we commend to the consolation of Thy Spirit, and the guardianship of Thy love, — we pray that they may dwell in the hearts of this people, that they may lie close to the consciences of this nation, and that to us and to generations that come after us they may ever be a guide and inspiration, an incentive to love what is good, to do what is right, and to strive for all things noble and pure.

O our Father, sanctify unto this country this appointment of Thy Providence. Grant that the life, the

5

character, the services, and the death of our lamented
President may exert a holy influence, and may serve
to bind the hearts of all our people in all quarters of
this great Republic closer together in the bonds of
patriotic love and duty, so that our union may be
cemented in tender ties and sympathies; so that the
peace, the prosperity, the glory, the progress of this
nation may endure through long generations.

Almighty God, we commend to Thee thy servant,
the President of these United States, in the discharge
of the duties of the high position to which he has been
so solemnly called, and may all the scenes and circumstances under which he is called to it speak to his
heart and conscience, and make him wise and faithful.
May the sympathies and respect of the people go out
to him. May we remember all the difficulties and
perplexities and embarrassments that necessarily sur-
round him. May we refrain from harsh and hasty
judgments; may we wait and be patient, and do Thou
shed down upon him all the holy influences, and endue
him with the heavenly wisdom that shall make his
administration a blessing to this people, an honor to
himself, and a great good to the nation.

Bless, O God, we entreat Thee, this ancient and
venerable Commonwealth in all its dear and valuable
interests. Bless this City of our Fathers. Bless thy
servant, our Chief Magistrate, and all associated with
him in the management of our municipal affairs, and
help them so to conduct them as shall promote not
only our material prosperity, but our advancement in
manners, morals, institutions, and character, in all

things that shall serve to continue us a city set on a hill.

Bless all the peoples and nations of the world,—this great race of humanity struggling and striving here upon earth. Help each and all to subdue the evil in the individual heart, that thus an end may come to injustice and wrong. Teach the violent in all lands and in all classes that the wrath of man worketh not the righteousness of God. O our Father, bring all the customs, habits, institutions, all the thought and action of mankind, into a closer and closer harmony with the spirit, the character, the teachings of Him who, coming to bear witness to Thy truth, and to proclaim Thy love unto the world, bowed His head in a grand self-sacrifice on that cross from which He has shed pardon and peace, heavenly benedictions and holy influences, upon the world. In His name we offer our prayer, beseeching Thee to forgive our sins and to answer our prayers, and as His disciples we ascribe unto Thee the glory, the dominion, and the praise forever. Amen.

The BOYLSTON CLUB then sang the Choral Hymn "Integer Vitæ."

The MAYOR then introduced the Honorable NATHANIEL P. BANKS, who proceeded to deliver his address, which was listened to with close attention and frequently interrupted by applause.

At the conclusion the Boylston Club sang the Choral Hymn "What God doth Will":—

Let not thy life be spent in lamenting;
    Be still, if God decree;
So shall it be my will;
    So let it be.

Care not thou if to-morrow brings sorrow;
    Above thee reigns still the One
Who all hath done,
    And loves thee.

So now in all thy striving, thy thriving,
    Stand surely;
What God doth will,
    That call thou best.

The audience was then dismissed with a benediction pronounced by the Rev. Dr. LOTHROP.

THE EULOGY, BY NATHANIEL P. BANKS.

.

EULOGY.

Mr. Mayor, Gentlemen of the City Council, and Fellow-Citizens: —

It is but little more than a year since the 250th anniversary of the Settlement of Boston was fitly and grandly commemorated. When compared with the lives of men such a period seems long. It is but a span, a breath in the life of nations. *Urbi et Orbi* — the city and the universe — was a pregnant maxim of the seven-hilled city of Rome. The three-hilled city of New England may lift its crest with pride, whenever and wherever the capitals of ancient or modern Europe are honored. It has achieved for the elevation and liberty of man, in a few generations, with a few hundred acres of land, more than Athens or Rome, Paris or London, accomplished in as many centuries. What it has done by itself and for itself was for the universal family of man.

The sad and unnatural events that now bring us together recall some of the incidents connected with the birth, growth, aspirations, and triumphs, of the metropolis of Massachusetts.

The town of Watertown, where the American ancestors of the late President of the United States

were cradled, was incorporated at an even date with
Boston. It was its outpost, its military protector, its
fountain of supplies, and the overflow of emigration
from the restricted jurisdiction and territory of the
city was a never-failing source of population and
strength for the adjacent inland settlement — twinned
with her, both at a birth — in the beautiful valley of
the River Charles. Salem and Charlestown had earlier
done as much for Boston.

Boston was the metropolis and mart of the colony,
the seat of government, the centre and focus of
wealth, and Watertown the earliest and strongest of
its inland settlements, outranking for a period of years
all others, except Boston, upon an exact estimate of
its varied elements of wealth and strength.

The history of the Plymouth settlement of 1620,
which preceded the embarkation of the Massachusetts
colony, was blistered with the results of a bitter and
apparently relentless destiny, against which it would
have been scarcely possible for any people but the
Massachusetts Pilgrims and Puritans, strengthened by
the later colony of Massachusetts Bay, to have
secured a triumph like that which the Deity they
worshipped vouchsafed to them.

Its founders were refugees from England, exiles in
Holland, and gladly braved suffering and death in the
New World, for liberty of conscience and freedom to
worship God. For the first ten years of its existence
its growth was painful and slow, numbering but
three hundred souls in 1630.

The colony of Massachusetts Bay, with which

Plymouth was united, left the Old World under happier auspices. It was freighted with concessions and congratulations from the crown. The best men in England were ambitious to share its fortunes. Winthrop, Saltonstall, and Sir Henry Vane — "the sad and starry Vane" — were among its leaders, and such men as John Hampden, John Pym, Oliver Cromwell, and many others of that heroic type, were restrained from emigration at the moment of embarkation, by the order of the king. Four thousand families — twenty thousand souls — people of culture, capacity, and character; no decayed courtiers or adventurers, but merchants, seamen, husbandmen, and others, skilled in labor and devoted to the highest interests of man, — had landed at Boston in ten years from the foundation of the city.

Among them came, in 1630, Edward Garfield, the paternal ancestor of the late President of the United States. He was a man of gentle blood, of military instincts and training, possessing some property, and a thoughtful and vigorous habit of mind and body. The earliest record of his name in the annals of the colony indicated an origin from some one of the great German families of Europe, and his alliance by marriage with a lady of that blood and birth confirmed the original impression of the people with whom he identified his fortunes as to his nationality. His emigration suggested a purpose consistent with his capacity and character, in harmony with the higher aspirations of the colony. He coveted possession of land, and for that reason probably, among others, settled in Watertown,

6

where territory was abundant, and boundary lines yet delicate and dim, especially toward the west, where they were mainly defined by the receding and vanishing forms of the aboriginal inhabitants of the country. In the realm they had abandoned it was a maxim among men, that home was where the heart was. But in the New World the colonists had discovered that both home and heart are where there is liberty and land.

He chose a residence near Charles river, a stream unsurpassed in beauty by any water that flows, since honored by the residence and immortalized by the verse of Longfellow, and the original and marvellous industries that enrich its peaceful and prosperous people.

Edward Garfield, the founder of this new American family, did not long linger near the boundaries of Boston. His first share in the distribution of land to the freemen, by the town, was a small lot or homestall of six acres of the territory afterwards incorporated as the town of Waltham. Another general grant of land by the town, in 1636, "to the freemen, and all the townsmen then inhabiting," one hundred and twenty in number, called the Great Dividends, gave to Garfield a tract of thirty acres, the whole of which was within the boundaries of Waltham. In 1650 the land allotted to Mr. Phillips, the first minister of Watertown, about forty acres, in the same locality, was sold, by his heirs, to Garfield and his sons. A portion of this estate was afterwards purchased from the heirs of Garfield by Governor Gore, who constructed upon it, from imported plans and materials, on his return from England, a country-seat, still admired as one of the most elegant and stately residences in America. The first distinctive title given to the territory embraced within the limits of Waltham was that of " The Precinct of Captain Garfield's Company." Captain Benjamin Garfield, whose name was thus honorably identified with that precinct, where he lived and died, was one of the distinguished men of his time. He held his military commission from the Governor of the colony. He was nine times Representative to the General Court, and often appointed Selectman and to other important offices. His monument, in the ancient cemetery of Waltham, still attests his high character and standing among the founders of Massachusetts. After the incorporation of that town this name rarely appears on the records of Watertown. While citizens of Watertown Garfield and his descendants were assigned to important military commands by the Governors of the colony, and frequently chosen to responsible town offices. Others were honored in a similar manner in Watertown, in Waltham, and wherever they planted themselves. They did not hive in the settled and safe centres of the colony, but struck out boldly for the frontier, where danger was to be encountered, and duty performed. They adhered zealously to the principles of the colony, and the controversies that arose from considerations of that nature, at the very outset of its history, settled upon an unchangeable basis the liberal character of the government of Massachusetts.

An important and instructive illustration of this free spirit of the people occurred in the second year of its history. Without previous consultation of the several towns, the Governor and assistants levied upon them, in 1632, an assessment of eight pounds sterling for construction of military defences in what is now Cambridge. This order was declared to be subversive of their rights. The people of Watertown, the most populous and influential inland town, met in church, with their pastor and elders, according to their custom, and, after much debate, deliberately refused to pay the money, on the ground, they said, "that it was not safe to pay monies after that sort, for fear of bringing themselves and their posterity into bondage."

When summoned before the Governor they were obliged to retract their declaration and submit. But they set on foot such an agitation through the colony as to secure, within three months of the original debate, an order for the appointment of two persons from each town to advise with the Governor and assistants as to the best method of raising public moneys. This order ripened, in 1634, into the creation of a representative body of deputies elected by the people, having full power to act for all freemen, except in elections. This was the origin of the House of Representatives in Massachusetts. After ten years' contest the council of assistants to the Governor was separated from the body of deputies, and, sitting as a Senate, left to the deputies chosen by the towns an absolute negative upon the legislation of the colony. Thus was established, substantially as it now exists, the Legislature of Massachusetts.

As the people began to be represented in the government of the colony, so the direction of civil affairs in the towns was intrusted to a municipal body of freemen, peculiar to New England, chosen for that purpose, and known as the Board of Selectmen. It is a satisfaction to know that, during the violent contests of ten years for this right of representation in State and local governments, Edward Garfield, the earliest American ancestor of the Martyr President whose loss we mourn, as selectman of Watertown, in the very crisis of that contest, did a freeman's duty with a freeman's will, in securing to the people of Massachusetts the rights of local and general representation they now enjoy.

The Massachusetts family of Garfields, in the male line, were churchmen, freemen, fighting men, thoughtful thrifty men, and working men. They were enterprising, active, and brave, fond of adventure, distinguished for endurance and strength, athletic feats, sallies of wit, cheerful dispositions, and, like their eminent successor so recently passed away, noted always for manly spirit and a commanding person and presence. It was a prolific and long-lived race. Marriages were at a premium, and families were large and numerous. Among the people of the Massachusetts Colony who made their way quickly to the frontier when new towns were to be planted, the Garfields were well represented. The foundation of a new municipality was then a solemn affair, usually preceded by

"a day of humiliation, and a sermon by Mr. Cotton."
When the territory of Massachusetts was overstocked
they passed to other States in New England, and
ultimately to the great West. Wherever they were
they asserted and defended the principles they inherited
from the founders of Massachusetts.

Abram Garfield, of the fifth generation, a minute-man
from Lincoln, engaged in the combat with the British
at Concord, in 1775, and was one of the signers of a
certificate, with some of the principal citizens of that
town, declaring that the British began the fight.
We should not feel so much solicitude about that
matter now.

Abram Garfield, a nephew of the soldier at Concord,
whose name he bore, who represented the seventh
generation of the family, settled later in Otsego County,
New York, where he received the first fruits of toil as
a laborer on the Erie canal. The construction of
canals by the government of Ohio drew him, with
other relatives, to that State, where his previous experience gained for him a contract on the Ohio canal.
The young men and women who left the earlier settlements for frontier States sometimes consecrated the
friendships of their youth by a contract of marriage
when they met again in the great West. Abram Garfield in this way met and married (February 3, 1821)
Eliza Ballou, a New Hampshire maiden, whom he had
known in earlier years. It was a long wait, and a
solid union. They were nearly twenty years of age
when married. A log cabin with one room was their
home. His vocation was that of an excavator of

canals in the depths of the primeval forests of Ohio. There was not much of hope or joy in the life before them; but still it was all there was for them of hope or joy. They could not expect the crown of life until they had paid its forfeit. They adhered to the religious customs of childhood. Their labor prospered. Amid their suffering and toil in the construction of the arteries of civilization, and the foundation of states and empires that will hereafter rule the world, four children came to bless them. The last was JAMES ABRAM GARFIELD (Nov. 19, 1831), destined, in the providence of God, to be, and to die, President of the Republic of the United States.

When he was less than two years of age his father died. But the orphan boy had no cause of fear. His heroic mother strode, axe in hand, into the primeval forest; felled trees, split rails, set posts, enclosed grain-fields. The elder children stood sentry by her side, or gave her their feeble aid. Soon the youngest child — he who was to be President — engaged in the rude employments of the vicinage. He burned wood for ashes, made potash and pearlash; drove mules on the tow-path of the canal, became deck-hand, and read in the stars at night legends of the bright future before him,— an innocent and inexpensive delight that was never at any period of his life denied him. Ten long years of toil, building canals, felling forests, clearing lands, cutting roads, fencing fields, diplomatizing with Indians, fighting wolves and resisting the avarice and brutality of civilization, left upon their bleached cheeks many traces and tears of agony.

Those were sad words with which the Roman poet described the origin and growth of the Eternal City. *Tantæ molis erat, romanam condere gentem!* How much rough work it cost to build Imperial Rome! There is a sigh in every letter and anguish in every word of that touching epitome of the history of the world, and the widowed mother and her orphan children learned at what cost, of hearts' blood, states are formed and empires founded. It was a mother's heart that at length suggested — always to the right child — a more thorough instruction, and a teacher's vocation for the youngest boy. Nations must be enlightened, though their foundations are cemented with blood. Some private instruction, the seminary at Chester, and the college at Hiram, founded by the Church of the Disciples, to which the mother and son adhered, opened a path to this higher destiny. The college at Bethany, of the same faith, was proposed when earlier courses were completed. But the blood within the boy, the living blood of his ancestors, turned his steps to the universities of New England, which gave him new elements of life, enlarged the circles of enduring friendship essential to his success, and engrafted the refinements of an older civilization upon the vigorous stock and stem of the western world.

And so, in 1856, he graduated at Williams College in Massachusetts. Returning to the West, he was again, for about five years, Professor and President at Hiram College. During this period, though not regularly ordained, he officiated as a preacher of the gospel.

Great events were then ripening, and his active spirit panted for a wider field of action. The opening of the civil war, in 1861, found him a senator in the Legislature of Ohio. The call for troops, after the first battle of *Bull Run*, made him a colonel of the forty-second Ohio Volunteers. The battle of Prestonburg gave him a brigadier-general's commission. Gallant and meritorious services at Chickamauga brought him merited promotion and the rank of major-general. The next year (1862) he was chosen a member of Congress, as successor of Joshua R. Giddings, of the Western Reserve, a dauntless and deathless champion of universal emancipation and liberty, and he accepted that seat in Congress, made vacant by death, upon the urgent recommendation of President Lincoln and prominent members of his cabinet. This ended his connection with the army as an officer. He served as a member of the House for eight successive terms.

In January of last year (1880) he was chosen Senator of the United States for Ohio, and in November of the same year elected by the voluntary suffrages of his countrymen President of the Republic. Such a flush and flood of peaceful triumphs were rarely before united in one man.

He was inaugurated the 4th day of March, with manifestations of satisfaction and harmony never before exhibited. He completed the organization of the government with like success. On the morning of the 2d day of July, at the moment of leaving the capital for a visit to the homes of his ancestors in Massachusetts, the scenes to which reference has been made,

7

he was assassinated, dying the 19th day of September, at Elberon, New Jersey, whither he was borne in the vain hope of relief. So fair and foul a day we have not seen.

For eighty days the civilized world waited with alternations of hope and fear the final result. Never before, it may be said without exaggeration, was such sorrow manifested, such tokens of sympathy extended, such universal prayers offered by individuals and nations, as for the relief and recovery of the suffering President.

Undoubtedly the open assertion in some parts of the world of the right of assassination as a method of reform in administration and government, may have intensified the general interest in this calamitous event. But the courage and composure with which the presidential martyr bore his affliction; the firmness and constancy of his aged mother; the serenity and saint-like resignation of a heroic wife, administering consolation and courage to husband and father, with a voice sweet as the zephyrs of the south, a spirit gentle as love, and a soul dauntless as the souls of women in Israel, — were not unobserved or unhonored. It melted hearts in the four quarters of the globe, and drew from the sons of men, in every land and clime, such attestation and confession of the faith that all created beings are children of one Father, as never before fell from human lips. We should be dead to sensibility and honor did we not feel such unwonted tests of the universal sweep and scope of human sympathy vouchsafed to us by the appointed leaders of churches, empires, and republics; and by that august lady, the Queen of England and Empress of India, that presides over the councils of the empire whence we derive our ideas of Christian faith, language, liberty, and law, who gave to the afflicted children of revolted and Republican America the emblems of mourning, reserved by the customs of her court to the best beloved and bravest of her realm, sending, by her own hand, to wife, mother, and orphans, swift and touching evidence of the strength of her sympathy and the depths of her sorrow, — the grandest of sovereigns and noblest of women!

We turn from this record of active and honorable service to a brief consideration, such as the occasion permits, of the elements of character which distinguished President Garfield. After all, character is the only enduring form of wealth. It is the power by which the world is ruled, the only legacy of true value that can be transmitted to posterity.

Let us glance for a moment at some of the principal events of the last fifty years, — a full half century, — from 1831 to 1881.

President Garfield was born in 1831. South Carolina had then announced her purpose to annul certain laws of the United States within her own jurisdiction: that is to say, certain laws of the United States were to be regarded in that State as of no validity or legal force; and this by the act of the State alone, without consultation or consideration with or for the

United States. In other States the laws of the government were to be obeyed, unless one or all of those States, following the example of South Carolina, should annul them. This action contemplated the overthrow and destruction of the authority of the general government within that State; and from that day to this, in one form or another, the intent and purpose of the nullifiers of the South to cripple or destroy the power of the United States, so far, at least, as to render it innocuous and inoffensive to persons who did not like it, its legislation, or its theories, was never entirely abandoned.

The process of nullification was directed ostensibly against the tariff legislation of that period, but in fact, as afterwards admitted, it was to protect and perpetuate slavery, and to establish a theory of government under which any State could annul laws of the United States on that subject. This phase of the doctrine of State sovereignty was overthrown by the vigor and courage of President Jackson. He gave vent to his indignation against that treasonable heresy, and let loose his passions upon its agents in, as he thought, his native State, for their attempt to overthrow the government of which he was the head. It was then universally believed that the doctrine of State supremacy was dead. But it does not so appear now.

In 1852 Mr. Garfield came to the full age of manhood. He found the doctrine of State suprem-acy in apparent discredit, and nullification absolutely discarded. The object at that time was — assuming that the Constitution was intended to protect slavery, but had from some cause or other failed to do it—to induce Congress to establish, by constitutional compromises, doctrines in regard to slavery which neither the Constitution, nor the framers of the Constitution, ever entertained, to wit, that the supremacy of slavery should be established by irrevocable and unchangeable laws, enacted by Congress.

This would produce, by affirmative legislation of Congress, the same results that would have followed the negative method of nullification by States. It would have established the supremacy of slavery and the destruction of the government as a national institution. Andrew Jackson did not then stand at the helm. The compromise was made a law in 1850, and endorsed in the presidential election of 1852.

The subject of slavery was forever to remain unchallenged and unopposed by the national government. Political conventions endorsed it as a finality in legislation on that subject. The Senate Committee of Territories, with a majority of Southern members, declared that to open the question of slavery, so solemnly settled, by the repeal of the Missouri compromise, or otherwise, would deluge the land in blood. The President announced that any action of that character would meet his official disapproval. The country had, in fact, surrendered to the demand for congressional recognition of the supremacy of slavery and the slave States over the national government! Nevertheless, the question was immediately opened by the same power that had so recently closed it. The sacred compact and compromise of 1850 was broken. The Missouri Compromise of 1820 was repealed, and the monstrous doctrine proclaimed, by the highest judicial tribunal, as an interpretation of existing laws, that four million people of the United States, who might become twenty millions, "had no rights a white man was bound to respect." This was the second epoch in that important history, and of the career of the late President.

In 1860 Garfield was a Senator of the Ohio Legislature; in 1862 a Major-General of the army, and in 1863 a member of Congress. Abraham Lincoln had been inaugurated President of the United States. The nullifiers threatened secession. Thirty years earlier they had attempted the nullification of certain laws of the United States, within the States. Now they proposed to nullify all laws and repudiate all authority of Congress, within the States, and to eject the general government from its jurisdiction and territory. The friends of the government deprecating war, and fearing a dissolution of the Union, adopted, by immense majorities, in Congress, an amendment of the Constitution declaring that no legislation affecting slavery should ever be proposed by the free States, leaving that vexed question entirely to the tender mercies of slave-holders. But it did not prevent secession, nor avert war. Most of the slave States withdrew from the Union. War was declared. A fratricidal contest of four years ensued. The confederate armies surrendered; peace was established; the States returned to the Union, slavery was abolished, and the emancipated slaves invested with the right to vote and hold office, — a third memorable epoch in this history.

At the death of President Garfield, during the last month, the great political organizations of the country, substantially the same as before and since the war, held an exact or nearly equal balance of power in every political division of the government except the executive department. The Senate was exactly balanced, and without power to act on political questions unless some senator abandoned his own to give a majority to the opposing party. The House of Representatives was in a similar condition of incapacity to act, except by affiliations and combinations of opposing factions. The States nearly balanced each other, and the popular vote, at the election of 1880, did not show a majority of more than three or five thousand votes on one side or the other. The government was at a dead-lock, — an embrace of death if indefinitely continued. And this is the substantial result of a perpetual conflict of half a century to preserve the government of the Republic !

It sometimes occurs, at the close of great trials, that reaction gathers courage and strength, and progress, wearied with contest, or satiated with victory, pants for breath, and finds in rest, spirit and power for possibly greater efforts and grander triumphs. Such is, perhaps, the secret of the present situation. But upon what glorious results this reaction follows ! The past half century is the epoch of emancipation. Millions of slaves have been invested with the prerogatives of liberty by England, France, the United States, and Russia, —

four of the great empires of the globe branding the
petty remnants of chattel slavery everywhere with in-
effaceable signs of decay and death. With this great
epoch of emancipation the late President rose from
obscurity to fame. He gave to its work, in sunshine
and shadow, his affection and strength. Upon him, at
its close, though not its first or greatest leader, rested
its highest honors, and the tragic termination of his
life seals forever the union of his name and fame with
its imperishable triumphs.

We know how much the character of one age is
affected by that which precedes it. The early
colonial history of Massachusetts left its impress
upon his spirit. The suffering and sorrows of his
immediate ancestors were not lost upon him. Like the
most pleasing of Milton's deities he had

> Much of his father, but of his mother more;

and it was undoubtedly upon the record of events in
the last half century of our political history that he
was led, from the opening of his career, to devote
himself to the active studies and duties of public life;
for we know that, whether or not he aspired to the
high station he reached, he was eminently well prepared for it. The rubric of events so briefly sketched,
measured by days and hours, as by thought and deed,
was the exact term, division, and limit of his life. He
knew and comprehended it. Upon it his character
was founded.

He could not have failed to observe that the pres-
ervation of the Union was an object of the highest

possible importance, over and above all others; that
every act of legislation proposed in the interest of
slavery imperilled to the extent of its success the
authority and existence of the Union, and that unyield-
ing resistance alike to direct and indirect assaults upon
its integrity and authority was the highest duty of .
every citizen. This was his platform. To it he gave
the best efforts of his life. In the early part of our
history, Southern leaders of the Union—Washington,
Jefferson, Madison, Monroe, and many others—hoped
and believed that slavery would become extinct· through
the influence of the Constitution and the force of natural laws. The contest made against the authority of
the Union in 1832 put an end to that expectation.
The Compromise act of 1850, and the Kansas and
Nebraska act of 1854, not only disposed of all such
theories, but established the supremacy of slavery
over government and people. Previous to this legislation, and the Dred Scott decision of 1857, the institution presented mainly an abstract question, whether
or not, on the whole, slavery was permissible or excus-
able, expedient or just, which allowed many conscien-
tious and Christian persons to hesitate in declaring
against it, and many more to avoid opinion or action.
When the recognition of slavery compelled an unre-
served approval of that compromise, the Fugitive Slave
law, the repeal of the Missouri Compromise against
slavery, an abrogation of the power of Congress to
legislate upon that subject, which it had exercised
with the approval and consent of all the slave States
for fifty years, and an assent to the judicial interpre-

tation of the Constitution and laws by the Supreme Judicial Court of the United States, which declared that slaves "had no rights which the white man was bound to respect"; and that "negroes might justly and lawfully be reduced to slavery for his benefit"; when Congress and the Supreme Court had annulled all legal and constitutional power of the government and people, inconsistent with this white man's decree, then slavery was no longer an abstraction. It became a practical matter, involving the rights of all classes, and the existence of the government. While it was considered an abstraction, slavery was arrogant, aggressive, triumphant. When freedom became a practical matter, involving the existence of their government, the people assumed the offensive, and won victories commensurate with the dignity and justice of their cause. The momentary triumph of slavery was its destruction, and it must have been sport for old Homer's gods, if any still live, to see these engineers "hoist with their own petard."

Garfield came to the full age of manhood, and gave his first vote, in the very year when the legislation of Congress, with constitutional interpretations of the Supreme Court, had made the Constitution a bulwark of slavery and the slave power.

Doing no injustice to multitudes of intelligent and patriotic young men of the country, and considering only the eminence he had attained at his death, we may imagine him perhaps to have been an unconscious and unrecognized leader of the new recruits, in the great electoral contests of 1854, 1856, and 1860, which established the supremacy of the constitution and liberty! Garfield, Fremont, and Lincoln! What memories surge from the depths of the past at the mention of their names! No political contests ever involved more important and vital issues, from the beginning of government. No forces were ever better marshalled; no victory better deserved; no triumph more complete!

There was singular force and strength in a declaration made by the pastor of the Disciples' Church, at the burial service of President Garfield. The funeral obsequies were celebrated — for the first time in the history of the Republic — in the rotunda of the capitol at Washington. The gigantic proportions of this apartment excite a profound sensation in every visitor. One familiar with the scene recalls at his entrance an ancient tradition, often repeated before the war, that this majestic central building of the capitol was at some day to witness the coronation of a king. Apart from the unusual solemnity of the ceremonies the scene was of an extraordinary character. The light that fell from the dome above gave a solemn aspect to the apartment. Distinguished personages moved silently and slowly to the positions assigned them. Two ex-Presidents, immediate predecessors of the deceased, the only occupants of the presidential office ever present on such occasion, sat in front of the eastern entrance of the rotunda. The Diplomatic Corps, in full court costume, were placed in rear of the ex-Presidents. Senators, judicial officers in their robes, officers of the army and navy in brilliant uniforms, were on the right. Members and ex-members of the

House, in large numbers, attended by the Speaker, were massed upon the left, and the space around them was crowded by distinguished citizens from every part of the country. The august assembly rose as the President, with cabinet officers and the stricken family of mourners, passed to their seats near the casket of the deceased Chief Magistrate, — resting upon the same bier that bore the body of President Lincoln, just beneath the centre of the canopy that from the dome overhangs the rotunda, and guarded by veterans of the army of the Cumberland. The walls were hung with representations of soul-stirring events in American history: the landing of Columbus, De Soto's discovery of the Mississippi, the baptism of Pocahontas, the embarkation of the Pilgrims, the Declaration of Independence, the surrender of Cornwallis at Yorktown, and the resignation of Washington. On the belt of the rotunda above were seen Cortez entering the Temple of the Sun in Mexico, the battle of Lexington, and other studies of immortal themes in the history of the Republic.

Simple, brief, and impressive ceremonies heightened the deep and general interest of the occasion. The funeral discourse was of a purely religious character, with scarcely more than a brief allusion to the career of the deceased President, and no mention, I think, of his title or his name. But these omissions intensified the general interest in the brief personal allusions. "I do believe," the preacher said, "that the true strength and beauty of this man's character will be found in his discipleship of Christ!"

It is not my province to speak of the spiritual character of this connection, but in another relation I believe it is true.

The Church of the Disciples, to which he belonged, is one of the most primitive of Christian communions, excluding every thought of distrust, competition, or advantage. It gave him a position and mission unique and generic, like and unlike that of other men. While he rarely or never referred to it himself, and might have wished at times, perhaps, to forget it, he was strengthened and protected by it. It was buckler and spear to him. It brought him into an immediate communion — a relation made sacred by a common faith, barren of engagements and responsibilities — with multitudes of other organizations and congregations, adherents and opponents, able and willing to assist and strengthen him, present or absent, at home or abroad, who dismissed aspersions upon his conduct and character as accusations of Pharisees against a son of the true faith, and gave him at all times a friendly greeting and welcome, whenever and wherever he felt inspired to give the world his thought and word. All great movements and revolutions of men and nations are born of this spirit and power.

In another direction the deceased President possessed extraordinary capacities. He was animated by an intense and sleepless spirit of acquisition. It was not, apparently, a sordid thirst for wealth, precedence, or power, which stimulates many men in our time. His ambition was for the acquisition of knowledge. From early youth to the day of his last illness it was a consuming passion. He gave to it days and nights, the strength of youth, the vigor of middle age. When in the forests of New York he made the rocks and trees to personate the heroes of his early reading. Engaged in the duties of his professorship he found time for other studies than those prescribed by the faculty, and for lectures, addresses, and many other intellectual pursuits. He studied law while at college, without the knowledge of his intimate friends, until he was admitted to the bar. When in Congress he would frequently occupy a whole night in examination of questions to be considered the next day, and debate them as if nothing unusual had occurred.

Setting aside all scruples, he would remain weekdays or Sundays in the Library of Congress whenever public duties required it. This capacity for labor gave him manifold and vast advantages over other men incapable of such toil. It was his stronghold. This was perceptible in the first instance in his connection with the army during the civil war.

At the opening of that memorable contest there were many men suddenly summoned from the pursuits of civil life, and unaccustomed to preparations for war, who were necessarily incapable of suggesting the best methods of organization, and for that reason unable at once to enter upon a career of positive, well-considered, and resolute activity; and some, at least, of those who had been instructed by the government in the mystery and art of scientific warfare, after a long and familiar dalliance with "the canker of a calm world and a long peace," were only fired with the rash enthusiasm of indolence and inactivity. This inexperience cost the government much precious time, which, otherwise applied, might have put an end to the war before it was begun. In great emergencies there are always many useless men of genius and learning; but, in administration and government at least, men of labor are scarce and invaluable. Garfield was one, and a leader among them. When he entered the army he did not wait for orders, but began to learn first what was to be done, and then how to do it. It was his rôle, the ordinary habit of his life. He had but just entered the field of war at the opening of the campaign in Kentucky, when necessity compelled him to resume his laborious habits of school and college. He set himself at work to learn, as best he might, what was in the wind; where was the enemy, what his strength, and how best to fight or evade him. It was easy for him to digest information picked up in many weeks' inquiry, and mass its details under appropriate heads, which, when applied to the objects immediately in view, presented, in itself, an effective and complete plan of operations without study or trouble. This was less the result of special capacity than of general habits of industry, a love of labor, and a burning thirst for acquisition and information.

And so, later in the war, when he became Chief-of-Staff of the Army of the Cumberland, under General Rosecrans, — which was the post he chose, and then undoubtedly the appropriate field for him, — we learn, upon good authority, that his bureau of military information was the most perfect machine of the kind organized in the field during the war. And when, at last, an advance upon the enemy became necessary to satisfy an impatient government and people, and seventeen generals, whose opinions were asked by Rosecrans, advised against the movement, their reports were submitted to Garfield for examination. He analyzed them, contrasted the views of one with those of another, compared their results with complete reliable and varied intelligence acquired from his officers, scouts, spies, the southern people, fugitives, contrabands, and the movements of the enemy, and, in a complete analysis and study of the situation, upon information which he alone presented, and against the opinion of nearly all subordinate generals, reduced to demonstration the truth of his premises and conclusions, and led the way to the Tullahoma campaign, which is said to have been as perfect in plan and as ably executed as any campaign of the war. In speaking of the report, Whitelaw Reid, in his history, "Ohio in the War," says: "This report we venture to pronounce the ablest military document known to have been submitted by a chief-of-staff to his superior officer during the war."

Garfield had, also, preëminent skill in directing and applying the labor and attainments of others to the success of his own work. This is a somewhat rare, but an invaluable capacity. No one man can do everything. In labor, as in war, to divide is to conquer. There have been men who knew everything and could do everything, — whose incomparable capacities would have been sufficient, under wise direction, to have given the highest rank among the few men that have changed the destiny of the world; but who could not succeed in government, because they never saw men until they run against them.

Such admirable qualities, united to such strength and love for active service, gave him reputation and rank, and opened the way to brilliant campaigns in Kentucky against Marshall at Prestonburg and at Middle Creek, — the last a cause of other victories elsewhere, — and at Tullahoma and Chickamauga.

His knowledge of law, privately acquired, opened a new field of activity and service, of great benefit to him and the government. But little attention had been given by professors of legal science, at the opening of the war, to the study of military law. In the field where it was to be administered, great difficulties were encountered in determining what the law was, and who was to execute it. A distinguished jurist, Dr. Francis Lieber, was appointed by the government to codify and digest the principles and precedents of this abstruse department of juridical science. But it opened to Garfield, long before the digest was completed, a peculiar field for tireless research and labor in new fields of inquiry. Once installed as an officer of courts-martial his services were found to be indispensable. From the West he was called to Washington, entered immediately into confidential communication with President Lincoln in regard to the military situation in Kentucky, was a member of the most important military tribunals, became a favorite and protegé of the Secretary of War, and, by express wish of the President and Secretary, accepted a seat in the House of

Representatives, to which he had been chosen in 1862.

His career in Congress is the important record of his life. For that he was best fitted; with it he was best satisfied; in it he continued longest, and from it rose to the great destiny which has given him a deathless name and page in the annals of the world.

The House of Representatives, in the age of Clay, Calhoun, and Webster, was an institution quite unlike that of our own time. Its numbers then were small, its leading men comparatively rare; but few subjects were debated, and members of the House seldom or never introduced bills for legislative action. Its work was prepared by committees, upon official information, and gentlemen wishing to speak upon its business could always find an opportunity. Now its numbers have been doubled. More than ten thousand bills for legislative consideration are introduced in every Congress. The increase of appropriations, patronage, and legislation is enormous, and the pressure for action often disorderly and violent. Little courtesy is wasted on such occasions, where one or two hundred members are shouting for the floor; and when one is named by the Speaker it must be a strong man, ready, able, eloquent, to gain or hold the ear of the House. Garfield never failed in this. His look drew audience and attention. He was never unprepared, never tedious, always began with his subject, and took his seat when he had finished. He had few controversies, and was never called to order for any cause. He was a debater rather than an orator; always courteous, intelligent,

intelligible, and honorable.   The House listened to him
with rapt attention, and he spoke with decisive effect
upon its judgment.   He liked it to be understood that
he was abreast of the best thought of the time; he had
a high regard for the authority of scientific leaders,
and walked with reverential respect in the tracks of
the best thinkers of the age.   It is a pleasant thing,
this method of settling all problems by demonstration
of exact science.   Hudibras must have been in error
when he spoke so lightly of these scholastic methods,
saying, or rather singing: —

> That all a rhetorician's rules
> Teach him but to name his tools.

But there are moments when abstruse, scientific terms
leave an insatiate and aching void in the human heart.
Multitudes felt the sting of such a sorrow as they
watched, with agonizing interest, toward the close of
the President's suffering, his terrible struggle for life,
and trembled, with alternations of hope and fear, as
they studied the morning and evening bulletins that
described the incidents of night and day with the
precision of exact science in language freshly bor-
rowed from the medical terminology of ancient Greeks
and Egyptians, that seemed to impart new terrors to
disease and death.   And they turned with infinite relief,
though not always with strengthened hopes, to the
telegrams of the Secretary of State, announcing to the
world, in the language of common life, the changes
that had occurred in the ebb and flow of life's dark
tide.

As chairman or a prominent member of the principal business committees of the House, Garfield had an easy access to the floor, and an eager assembly as his audience. His topics were generally of a national character, connected with the organization and maintenance of various departments of the government; but there was scarcely any subject brought before Congress to which he had not at some time given a thorough and able exposition of his views. The best known and most influential of his speeches were in relation to the war, financial affairs, the currency, and the tariff. These all involved national interests, and exhibit on his part a profound study of every subject necessary to their support. He was from the first, and constantly, a hard-money man, a leader in discussion, and a supporter by his votes of every proposition necessary to maintain a sound currency. On the subject of the tariff, while he did not deny that, as an abstract question, the doctrine of free trade presented an aspect of truth, he always declared that under a government like ours protection of national industries was indispensable. He advocated duties high enough to enable the home manufacturer to make wholesome competition with foreigners, but not so high as to subject consumers to a home monopoly of product or supply. A moderate and permanent protection was the doctrine he always ably sustained. It would be instructive to recall the expression of his views embodied in his speeches upon these subjects, which he photographed upon the minds of those to whom they were addressed, but inappropriate at the present moment. His speeches on occasions of ceremony — to most persons difficult and embarrassing because of their departure from the usually impetuous and often stormy courses of debate — were numerous, and always classed with the best records of commemorative and æsthetic oratory.

Few men in the history of the House of Representatives have acquired a higher reputation, and none will be more kindly and permanently remembered.

It was said by one of the wisest of the ancient Greeks that it is "impossible to penetrate the secret thoughts, quality, and judgment of man till he is put to proof by high office and administration of laws." Whatever we may think of the splendid record of the late President in every walk of life he followed, it does not enable us to anticipate the character and ultimate success of the administration upon which he so happily entered. In other positions of public life the concurrence of so many different influences is required to accomplish even slight results, that individual credit or responsibility therefor is often slight and intangible. In the administration of government, the highest secular duty to which men are ever called, responsibility is indivisible and unchangeable; and the final results, whether for good or evil, are indelibly stamped on the woof and warp of the web of time, and will so remain forever. Good intentions are of no account, and a plea of confession and avoidance, — admitting failure but disclaiming error, — so advantageous in other cases, never influences the world in judging men who fail rightly and successfully to administer government. We are happy in being absolved from the responsibility of such judgment where authoritative decision is impossible.

Of his ideas of administration and government, their object, method, scope, and power, he has left a record which will forever stand a monument of his capacity and genius for investigation, discrimination, learning, a just comprehension of what should be required, and the best method of achieving desired results. His inaugural address is a masterly exemplification and vindication of his views, and the satisfaction with which it was received, an indication of the confidence of the country in his ability to execute purposes so wisely and well stated. But the vigor of war is not always equal to its sounding protocols.

A comparison of what he had done, with what he might do, would give assurance of splendid success. It was on that principle that the late presidential canvass terminated in his elevation and honor. He had been faithful in a few things; he was made ruler over many. But, beyond that, no tribunal is competent for a final decision, and judgment must be suspended. We have other duties more closely identified with his fame, and our success and happiness, that claim our attention.

What influences and what measures may be relied upon to avert the repetition and extension of this

terrible calamity which has again fallen upon the
Republic and its people — inexplicable, immeasurable,
and unnatural — is a subject of supreme importance,
possibly, of unconquerable difficulty.

To shield crime by false accusations of innocence will
not accomplish it. To attribute this calamity to causes
which are inseparable from liberty, which are inherent
in every free government, and from which this country
has never been and can never be free so long as liberty
exists, will neither protect us from further peril nor
absolve us from weighty and crushing responsibilities
now and hereafter.

The political complications and convulsions of the
present year are slight in comparison with those of
other periods of our political history, not in one city
or state, but in every city and state throughout the
country.

The city of Boston cannot have forgotten the riots
incited in her streets against Washington and the
measures of his administration. The men of this
generation have never known nor heard of such political
violence as that directed against Jefferson and the
measures of his administration. We ought not to
forget, even here, that against the administration of
Madison, the father of the Constitution, — a modest,
peaceful, timid, irresolute man, — we ourselves organized,
justified, and defended, a political convention in a
neighboring city, which was supposed to have contemplated resistance to the government of the United
States. I am myself old enough to have heard, in a
neighboring State, on a calm and beautiful Sunday

morning, influential and respectable citizens and church-
members say openly and seriously, in the presence of
many persons, of whom I was one, that they would
assist in the assassination of Andrew Jackson. And
this on account of his measures against the Bank
of the United States. If honorable and educated
Christian men of New England entertained such ideas
of Jackson, who had just then saved the government
from destruction by nullification, what must have been
said of him by the nullifiers themselves, in South
Carolina, where nearly every man was a nullifier, and
where, as was said of O'Connell —

A nation was in a man comprised ?

We cannot forget what occurred during the administration of Mr. Lincoln, or of his successor, Mr.
Johnson. We have witnessed no such political convulsions in our day. No one ever excused the
assassination of Mr. Lincoln on such grounds, or
could have counselled such violence against the chiefs
of earlier administrations. Neither can it now be
done, with truth or justice. Those who enlisted in
the opposition to past administrations were men whose
intellectual and moral natures restrained them from
the execution of purposes dictated by passion. Those
whose feeble intellects limit their moral responsibility
we must restrain or protect, and never palliate, by
thought or act, offences that, under other circumstances, might have endangered the life of any President
of the Republic! There is no cause or incitement
to crime in the political controversies of this year

that might not have occurred under any previous administration; and neither motive nor temptation, of any kind whatever, for such an ineffable and inexpiable crime as the murder of the mild, generous, warm-hearted, forgiving, and Christian Chief Magistrate, whose loss we mourn.

It is unwise and unjust that individual idiosyncrasies or conduct should be charged to political parties or people, or that the institutions and government of the country should be considered as inevitable, natural, proximate, or even incidental causes of such criminal acts. Liberty offers opportunity, but never justification, for crime.

Political assassination is not insanity. It proceeds often from temporary self-imposed infection and distemper of the mind. It is not necessarily limited to the reform of administrations and governments. It can as well be applied to the settlement of private affairs as to the overthrow of dynasties.

It is a phase of the doctrine of annihilation that has been applied to the reform of governments elsewhere by large classes of discontented people; and we now learn with astonishment that it is as applicable to our own free and just government as to the despotisms of the Old World. It is not now for us to speak of repression or retribution; but one of the many sovereign remedies for its evils is to avoid convulsions, private and public, restrain passion, suppress injustice, practise moderation in all things, and do no evil that good may come.

10

The year 1881 is the complement of the full half-century since the first open movement was organized for the control or destruction of our government. The lesson of this half-century, with all its trials, sacrifices, and triumphs, is that it is wise to maintain and defend the government of our country and its lawfully constituted authorities, whether or not we created them or like them. In the contemplation of this half-century can we find cause to wish the government had been overthrown? Or can we now wish it crippled, or destroyed?

The lesson of Garfield's life is an admonition to protect, perfect, and defend our government. His birth marks the period when it was first assailed by enemies domestic, and at the close of his career he gave his last hours of health and strength to improve and protect it. His last friend should give his last sigh to maintain it, not for his honor, which is untarnished, nor his glory, which is immaculate, but for his country, which still has perils to encounter, and liberties to defend for the benefit of mankind!

Mr. Mayor and Gentlemen of the City Government: —

The earthly career of the Chief Magistrate of the Republic is closed. The honors paid to his memory by the metropolis of Massachusetts, in accordance with its custom, are well bestowed. From city and universe his character challenges respect and honor! On the shore of the great lake, where he wished to rest, he sleeps well. Death separates us at the grave, and we make to him our last supreme adieu! What this sad and unnatural change portends to us, or our country, we know not. But for him, — our neighbor, compatriot, friend, brother, revered Chief Magistrate, — who came with us, as the Indian chief said to Washington, "out of this land," it brings limitless rest and peace. He has exchanged a few years of restless toil for a deathless fame. Except to fill the aching void of bruised hearts, who would recall him? He could not be assured of recognition or requital, though he might confer infinite blessings upon his country. "Detraction would not suffer it." Yet he would have gladly served his country in spite of the ingratitude of his contemporaries. For him "to die is gain." The word that most often and easily opens the portals of the realm of bliss is martyrdom. He fought a good fight; he finished his course; he kept the faith; he paid the penalty; he receives his reward according to the sacred presage and promise of God.

> " *E venni dal martirio a questa pace.*"
>
> These words the poet heard in Paradise,
>   Uttered by one who, bravely dying here,
>   In the true faith, was living in that sphere,
>   Where the Celestial Cross of sacrifice
> Spread its protecting arms athwart the skies;
>   And, set thereon, like jewels crystal clear,
>   The souls magnanimous, that knew not fear,
>   Flashed their effulgence on his dazzled eyes.
> Ah, me! how dark the discipline of pain,
>   Were not the suffering followed by the sense
>   Of infinite rest and infinite release!
> This is our consolation: and again
>   A great soul cries to us in our suspense, —
>   "I came from martyrdom unto this peace!"
>
> — *Longfellow.*

FINAL PROCEEDINGS.

FINAL PROCEEDINGS.

At a meeting of the Board of Aldermen, held on the 24th of October, 1881, Alderman CHARLES H. HERSEY offered the following resolutions, which were unanimously adopted : —

Resolved, That the thanks of the City Council be expressed to NATHANIEL P. BANKS, for the interesting historical sketch of the life and public services of JAMES A. GARFIELD, late President of the United States, which was eloquently presented by him before the City Council on the 20th instant, and that a copy thereof be solicited for publication.

Resolved, That the thanks of the City Council be tendered to the Directors of the Tremont Temple Association for their courtesy in allowing the City of Boston the free use of Tremont Temple, on the 20th instant, for the observance of the Memorial Services in honor of JAMES A. GARFIELD, the late President of the United States.

Resolved, That the thanks of the City Council be transmitted to the officers and members of the Boylston Club for their valuable assistance, which made so acceptable and so successful the musical portion of the Memorial Services, on the 20th instant, in honor

of JAMES A. GARFIELD, the late President of the
United States.

The Common Council, on the 27th of October, concurred in
the passage of the resolutions, and they were approved by the
Mayor October 28th, 1881.

www.ingramcontent.com/pod-product-compliance
Lightning Source LLC
Chambersburg PA
CBHW030004030726
47499CB00008B/2885